Peppa's Cruise Vacation

ISBN 978-1-338-88543-9

10 9 8 7 6 5 4 3 2 1   23 24 25 26 27

Printed in the U.S.A.   40

First printing 2023
Book design by Ashley Vargas

www.peppapig.com

SCHOLASTIC INC.

Granny and Grandpa Pig are taking Peppa and George on a cruise!

A cruise is a vacation on a big ship.

There are many ways to have fun on the cruise ship!

Peppa and her family can play on trampolines, swim in splash pools, and more.
But first, Peppa is ready to start her day with a big breakfast . . .

. . . at the Dinosaur Café! *Rawr!*
Everyone eats dinosaur breakfast eggs with spots on
them. They are delicious!

Pirate Pete and Mrs. Mermaid are at the Dinosaur Café, too.

"Ahoy there, sailors!" says Pirate Pete.

Mrs. Mermaid invites everyone to their evening show. It will be so much fun!

There is plenty of time to try other activities on the ship before the show.

George really wants to ride the potato.

George loves the ride so much, he doesn't want to try anything else!

"Tay-toe! Tay-toe!" George cheers again and again. The potato bounces back and forth.

Peppa wants to play on the trampolines. Rohan Rhino is bouncing there, too!

"Yippee!" they say. Peppa and Rohan jump and squeal until they get another idea for a fun way to spend the day.

Splash! Peppa and Rohan make waves as they slide into the mermaid splash pool.

"This is fun!" Peppa says as she splashes Rohan.
After a day of swimming, sliding, and splashing, Peppa can't believe it's already time for the big show!

Everyone wears a costume for the show. It's fun to dress up!

They take their seats, and the show begins . . .
Pirate Pete sails the seas looking for treasure, but he
can't find it on his own.

Mrs. Mermaid says she can help! She has a magic box that will give you whatever you wish for.

All it takes is the magic word.

"Abracadabra!" the crowd shouts together.

Poof! The chest is filled with chocolate coins. Pirate Pete tosses them to the crowd for everyone to enjoy!

But Mrs. Mermaid is nowhere to be found!

Peppa knows just what to do! She joins Pirate Pete on the stage.
"Abracadabra!" she says.

And Mrs. Mermaid returns!
Everyone claps and cheers. Thanks to
Peppa's help, it was a very magical show.

It has been a wonderful day! Peppa made new friends and tried new things. She even helped with the show!

George and Granny and Grandpa Pig have had a special day, too.
But there is still one more surprise before bedtime . . .

Splash!

That splash was much bigger than the one Peppa made in the mermaid splash pool! A friendly whale says, "Night night!" to everyone.

"Night night!" Peppa and George call back to the whale.

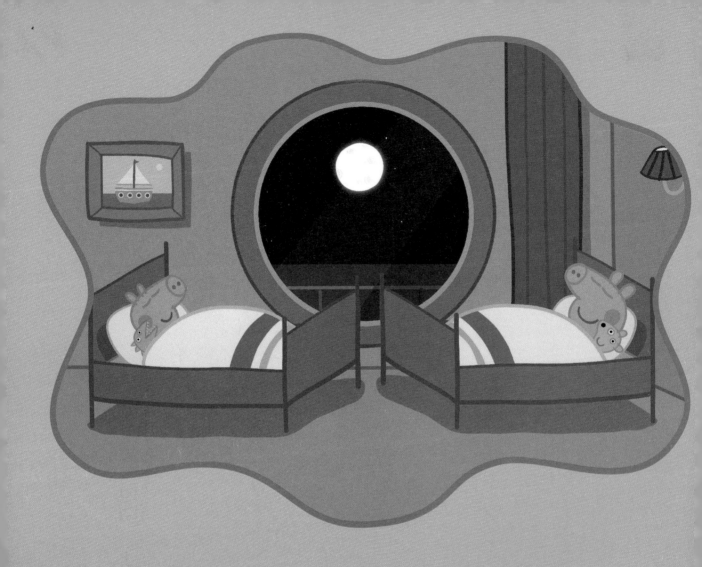

Tomorrow will be another fun-filled day at sea.